KRISPIN'S FAIR

LITTLE, BROWN & CO.   BOSTON · TORONTO

KRISPIN'S FAIR

BY JOHN G. KELLER

ILLUSTRATED BY ED EMBERLEY

FIRST EDITION

T 05/76

*Published simultaneously in Canada
by Little, Brown & Company (Canada) Limited*

PRINTED IN THE UNITED STATES OF AMERICA

Library of Congress Cataloging in Publication Data

Keller, John G.

Krispin's fair.

SUMMARY: A country fair teaches Prince Krispin and his haughty cousin a lesson in friendship.

[1. Friendship — Fiction] I. Emberley, Ed.
II. Title.
PZ7.K28134Kr.   [E]   76-3537
ISBN 0-316-48652-3

It was decided that
Prince Roderick would visit
his cousin, Prince Krispin.

Krispin rode out on Dumpling
to meet his cousin.
He saw at once that Roderick
was a very grand knight.

"It's so good to see you," Krispin said.

"I know," Roderick replied.

Krispin led Roderick to his castle.
Roderick found it small and plain.

For supper Krispin served
a good, hot meal.

But Roderick only
picked at his food.

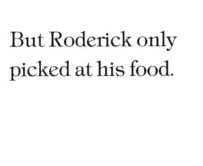

"You'll never guess what's
going to happen tomorrow," Krispin said
later that night. "It's a fair.
We're all going to have fun!

There will be good food,
singing, and turtle racing.
You do like turtle racing, don't you?"

"No!" Roderick growled.

Finally it was time for bed.

"Well, really!" Roderick sniffed.
"I am used to a feather bed,
and I am not used to beasts
in the bedroom."

Krispin left the castle.
It had not been a good day.

Krispin felt sorry for Dumpling,
and he felt sad about himself.
Most of all he felt angry with Roderick.
But what could he do?

Krispin looked at Dumpling
but Dumpling could not help him.
He thought and thought.
Finally he said to himself, "Krispin,
Roderick is a visitor, and you should be polite.
But he has no right to act the way he does.
Tomorrow is the fair. Are you going to enjoy
yourself, or are you going to feel sad again?
There's only one thing to do."
With that, he gave Dumpling a pat
and fell asleep.

"Ugh," grunted Roderick the next morning,
"the bed was much too lumpy, but at least
those creatures were outside,
so I did get a bit of sleep."

Krispin took a deep breath.
He looked his cousin in the eye.

"Roderick," he said, "I know things
may be much grander at the King's castle.
But this is home to me and I like it.
Now today we are going to have a fair.
My friends want to have a good time.
I want to have a good time, and, Roderick,
if you don't want to have a good time, too,
perhaps you should go home." And with that
Krispin went out to feed Dumpling.

Well! Roderick was a grand knight
and not used to that kind of talk.
At first he was very cross.

WELCOME!

BERRY
PIES!

But when he saw what fun everyone was having,
he decided to stay.

And he had a very good time indeed.

In fact, everyone had a very good time.